A Little Man with a Big Plan

The Story of Young David

Written and Illustrated by

Damon J. Taylor

FOR PARENTS
with Dr. Sock

This story will help children learn that God is with us always.

Read It Together–

The whole story of David and Goliath is in the Old Testament book of 1 Samuel 17.

Sharing–

Share a time from your childhood that would pertain to this story. Were you ever frightened by a bully? What did you do?

Discussion Starters–

• Has there been a time that you felt bullied?

• Who is it that knows our fears and wants to protect us?

• Do you think David ever felt fear on the battlefield?

• Was it wrong for David's brothers to be frightened by the giant?

For Fun–

Get a ladder from your garage, and stand on the step that would make you approximately nine feet tall. Tell your child that this is how tall Goliath was when David faced him in battle.

Draw–

Draw with your kids. Have them draw a picture of David and Goliath. David was about half the size of Goliath.

Prayer Time–

After reading the story, pray with your kids. Thank God for always being with them and protecting them from harm.

COLEMAN HAS FOUND THAT THE LIFE OF A LITTLE BOY

can be tough at times, especially if that boy has a baby sister named Shelby. When Shelby was born, Coleman needed a way to deal with his day-to-day problems. He found his socks. Yes, that's right, his socks.

It may seem weird, but these aren't your regular, everyday tube socks that you find in your dresser. As ordinary as they may appear, these socks really are Coleman's friends, and they help him with his problems. When life gets complicated, Coleman goes to his bedroom and works through his troubles by playing make-believe with his socks and remembering Bible stories he's learned.

So please sit back, take off your shoes and socks if you like, and enjoy Coleman's imaginary world in . . .

A Little Man with a Big Plan

The Story of Young David

Today has really become a busy day for Coleman.
First, he rescued his sister Shelby from Fang.

Then an even bigger and scarier challenge came up. . . .

Coleman's friend Bubba came over to play.

This wasn't really a problem, except for the fact that Bubba had grown tired of their regular games and created a new game called Let's Make Shelby Cry.

Coleman knew it was wrong for Bubba to take Shelby's blankie, but he had a hard time telling Bubba, "No."

"I'm twice as big as you are," Bubba reminded him.

"Come on, Coleman, let's play my new game and make Shelby cry! Or would you rather play Let's Make Coleman Cry?" Bubba ground his fist into his other hand.

Coleman was angry, but also afraid. He ran off to his room. He wanted to keep Bubba from sitting on him, and to figure out what to do.

He plopped down in front of a pile of his socks and started to play.

"Coleman, what are you doing?!" asked Sockariah, one of Coleman's sock buddies.

"You've left Shelby in the hands of that bully, Bubba!"

"What am I supposed to do, let Bubba pound on me too?" asked Coleman.

"No, I guess not," said Sockariah, "but don't you remember a guy from the Bible who had a similar problem? His name was David. . . ."

One day David was tending his flock when a lion attacked one of the sheep. David shook with fright, but he also knew that God was with him and would protect him.

He ran at the lion with a club, and snatched the lamb from its mouth.

The lion roared and lunged at him, but David grabbed it by the beard and killed it.
God had protected David and his sheep.

About that same time, David's brothers went off to war with the Philistines, mean people who didn't believe in God. The sneaky Philistines tricked the Israelites into making a deal with them.

"You send out your best warrior, and we will send out ours," they said. "Those two will battle to the death. Then everyone on the losers' side will become slaves of the winners. Do we have a deal?"

Little did the Israelites know, the Philistines had a trick up their sleeves—a secret weapon. And the secret weapon's name was . . .

GOLIATH,

a giant who stood over nine feet tall.
He was almost twice the size of Israel's
mightiest warrior, and twice as mean.

"Come out and fight me, you
Israelite dogs!" Goliath roared. "Is
there no one brave enough to fight me?
Are you all chickens? Bawk, bawk, bawk!"

The Israelite warriors hid in their tents. For days
and days this went on. Goliath paced the battlefield,
challenging the Israelites. And the Israelites ran
and hid.

On one of those days when the Israelites were hiding from Goliath, David's father called him in from the fields to take a lunch to his brothers at their camp.

David did as his father asked, and left to deliver his brothers' food.

When David arrived at the camp, he found his three older brothers and all the other soldiers hiding in their tents. They were shaking like leaves on a windy day.

"Hi, guys. How's the battle going?" asked David.

"SHHHHH! Quiet down," said one of his brothers. "Squeeze under a bed and hide before Goliath finds you."

Then they all heard a frightening sound. . . .

"Who will come and do battle with me, you Israelite dogs?" boomed Goliath. "Stop being such chickens, and come fight me!"

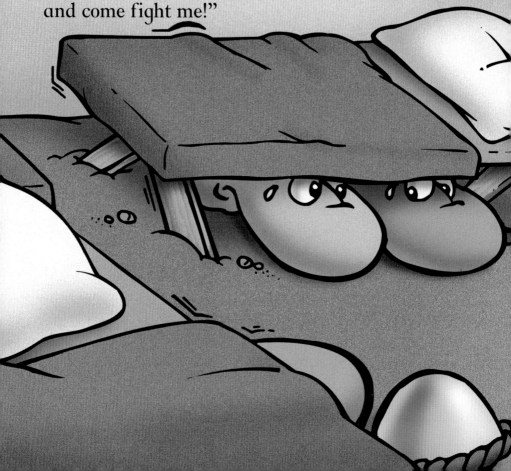

David stood up straight. "Who was that?" he demanded. "Who dares make fun of God's people and call God's army chicken?"

David rushed out of the tent and went directly to Israel's King Saul. David begged to be allowed to battle Goliath.

"You must be kidding," laughed King Saul.

"He would chew you up and spit you out, and we would all become slaves."

It took David a while to convince the king that he really could fight the giant, but the king eventually agreed.

King Saul gave his armor to David, but it was too big and clumsy. So David went to fight Goliath armed only with his sling and five smooth stones that he found in a nearby stream.

David marched out onto the battlefield.

"What's this?" shouted Goliath. "A boy? Are you all crazy? Are you such cowards that you send a boy to do a man's job?"

David ran at the giant and said, "I come in the name of the Lord Almighty!" He placed one stone in his sling. He swung it around and around over his head, and Whoosh!!!

He let go of the sling and the rock flew . . .

KONK!!!

The rock smacked Goliath right between the eyes. The giant fell dead! David had beaten him with his little sling. And with the help and protection of God, of course.

"So Coleman, did you learn anything from that story?" asked Sockariah.

"Yes, even way back then, no one liked being called a chicken," replied Coleman.

"Anything else?" asked Sockariah.

"I learned that David stood up to Goliath even though David was small. I need to stand up to Bubba. God will help me know what to say to him."

Coleman picked up his old blanket. "Where are you going with your old blankie, Coleman?" asked Sockariah. "I thought I'd give Shelby *my* blankie until Bubba goes home."

"Good idea, Coleman. Good idea."

The Child Sockology Series

<u>For ages up to 5</u>
Bible Babies
Bible Characters A to Z
Bible Numbers 1 to 10
Bible Opposites
New Testament Bible Feelings
Old Testament Bible Feelings

<u>For ages 5 and up</u>
A Little Man with a Big Plan: The Story of Young David
The Ark and the Park: The Story of Noah
Beauty and the Booster: The Story of Esther
Forgive and Forget: The Story of Joseph
Hide and Sink: The Story of Jonah
Lunchtime Life Change: The Story of Zacchaeus